IMAGINE THAT

Licensed exclusively to Imagine That Publishing Ltd
Tide Mill Way, Woodbridge, Suffolk, IP12 1AP, UK
www.imaginethat.com
Copyright © 2019 Imagine That Group Ltd
All rights reserved
2 4 6 8 9 7 5 3
Manufactured in China

Written by Jemima Summer
Illustrated by Emma Allen

ISBN 978-1-78958-301-4

A catalogue record for this book is available from the British Library

Hickory Dickory Dock

Jemima Summer
& Emma Allen

Hickory Dickory Dock,
The mouse ran up the clock.
The clock struck one,
The mouse ran down,
Hickory Dickory Dock.

Hickory Dickory Dock,
The mouse ran up the clock.
The clock struck two,
The mouse went 'boo!'
Hickory Dickory Dock.

Hickory Dickory Dock,
The mouse ran up the clock.
The clock struck three,
The mouse went 'whee!'
Hickory Dickory Dock.

Hickory Dickory Dock,
The mouse ran up the clock.
The clock struck four,
Mouse jumped to the floor,
Hickory Dickory Dock.

Hickory Dickory Dock,
The mouse ran up the clock.
The clock struck five,
Mouse did a jive,
Hickory Dickory Dock.

Hickory Dickory Dock,
The mouse ran up the clock.
The clock struck six,
Here come hen's chicks,
Hickory Dickory Dock.

Dong!

Hee hee!

Peep! Peep! Peep!

Zzz ...

Hickory Dickory Dock,
The mouse ran up the clock.
The clock struck seven,
Mouse found a melon,
Hickory Dickory Dock.

Hickory Dickory Dock,
The mouse ran up the clock.
The clock struck eight,
The mouse he ate,
Hickory Dickory Dock.

Hickory Dickory Dock,
The mouse ran up the clock.
The clock struck nine,
Mouse stood in line,
Hickory Dickory Dock.

Hickory Dickory Dock,
The mouse ran up the clock.
The clock struck ten,
And woke the hen,
Hickory Dickory Dock.

Hickory Dickory Dock,
The mouse ran up the clock.
The clock struck eleven,
It needed repairing!
Hickory Dickory Dock.

Hickory Dickory Dock.